THE EYE AND I

Weekly Reader Books Presents

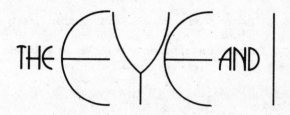

THE EYE AND I

Story by Lee Wardlaw
Illustrated by Kim Mulkey

Weekly Reader Books offers several exciting
card and activity programs. For information,
write to WEEKLY READER BOOKS, P.O. Box 16636
Columbus, Ohio 43216.

This book is a presentation of Weekly Reader Books. Weekly
Reader Books offers book clubs for children from preschool through
high school. For further information write to: **Weekly Reader
Books,** 4343 Equity Drive, Columbus, Ohio 43228.

Published by arrangement with Red Hen Press. Weekly Reader is a
federally registered trademark of Field Publications. Printed in the
United States of America.

LIBRARY OF CONGRESS CATALOGING-IN-PUBLICATION DATA

Wardlaw, Lee, 1955–
    The eye and I.

    Summary: Jeffrey's fear of the electronic eye of the video camera
nearly paralyzes him when he discovers he must make a filmed
speech before his fifth grade class, but then he comes up with a
sensational idea.
    [1. Stage fright—Fiction.   2. Schools—Fiction]
I. Stouffer, Deborah, 1950–   ill.   II. Title.
P27.W217Ey   1988   [E]   88-15664
ISBN O-931093-10-4

For the real Craig Zeisloft:
one hot surfer – L.W.

CHAPTER ONE

My fingers looked like lizards.

My toes looked like prunes.

I think I even saw a speck of mold growing in my belly button.

According to my waterproof watch with the Velcro band and digital read-out, I had been in the shower exactly 38 minutes, 42 seconds. I was shooting for the World's Record, and I'd make it for sure. See, I planned to stay in the shower the rest of my life. That way, I wouldn't have to go back to my 5th grade classroom and face The Eye.

I had just started shampooing my hair for the 12th time when I heard wham! wham! wham! on the bathroom door. I'd recognize those "whams" anywhere. They belonged to my sister Juliet. Juliet is 14. She wears sunglasses to school (even when it rains), falls in love at least four times a day, and has fingernails as long as California. She also has three favorite hobbies. They are:

1. Making my life miserable
2. Making my life miserable
3. Washing her hair.

I was using Juliet's shampoo right then. She could probably smell it under the door. It smells like fruit salad with coconut. I hate coconut. Why can't someone invent a shampoo that smells like peanut butter? I'd buy eighteen bottles of it in a second.

Wham, wham, wham!

Juliet sounded desperate.

"Who is it?" I called.

"Juliet. Hurry up! I need to use the bathroom."

"Juliet who?"

"What do you mean, 'Juliet who?' How many Juliets do you know?"

"Nine," I lied.

"Jeffrey, I'm going to be late for school. *You're* going to be late for school. So get outta there *now*. I need to wash my hair."

"I'm not coming out. Ever."

"Jeffrey McMillan, if you're not out of there by the time I count to ten, I'm telling Dad. Do you know what that means? It means you're history! Are you listening, Jeffrey?"

I lathered my hair with more "fruit salad" shampoo.

"Okay, Jeffrey. You asked for it! One, two, three..."

I sang a soap commercial.

"...four, five, six..."

I watched a sliver of soap whirlpool down the drain.

"seven, eight, nine - I'm warning you, Jeffrey! - okay, *ten*!" Juliet emphasized the number with another wham. "That's it, kiddo. I'm telling. You've had it now! I mean, *had* it! Daaaa-aaad,

Jeffrey won't get out of the show-werrr!"

I could hear Juliet screaming all the way down the hall. My sister's voice could shatter an armored tank.

I stuck my head under the shower nozzle and let the water roar over my ears. I didn't think about Juliet or school or The Eye. I pretended I was bathing in an African waterfall after a hard day of hacking through the jungle, hunting rhinoceros.

Someone knocked on the door.

"Who is it?" I called.

"It's Dad. How's the weather in there, son?"

"Wet," I answered. I thought of Africa. "And hot. Kind of tropical."

"Rumor has it that you're breeding mosquitoes."

"Not yet," I said, trying not to laugh. Dad's a writer. A funny one. Maybe someday he'll have a TV show like Bill Cosby.

"Jeffrey, I need to shave."

"I'm not coming out, Dad."

"Not ever?"

"No."

"Not even on your birthday?"

"Nope."

"Jeffrey, your skin will shrivel up and fall off."

Good, I thought. I can't go to school looking like *that*. My teacher, Miss Simmons, would be totally grossed out.

"Jeffrey, you've had your fun. But enough's enough now, hear me? I want you out of that shower by the count of ten. One...two..."

Why is it that no one in my family can count higher than ten?

A few minutes later, I heard another knock on the door.

"Who is it?" I called.

"It's Mom."

"I'm not coming out, Mom."

"Jeffrey, you have to come out. Your breakfast is ready. Two English muffins. And I stuffed the nooks and crannies with peanut butter, just the way

5

you like them."

"I'll eat them in here."

"They'll get soggy."

"Put them in a baggy."

"Oh, this is ridiculous!"

I heard a rattling noise, like someone messing around the door handle with a screw driver. Then the door opened. Steam swirled around me. An arm thrust through the opening of the shower curtain. Mom's arm.

"Hey!" I yelled. I tried to cover myself with a wash cloth. "Hey, I'm naked in here, you know!"

"I'm not looking at you, I'm looking for *this*." Mom's hand grabbed the faucet handle and wrenched off the water. "Besides, I'm your mother. I used to diaper you, remember?"

"No, I don't. Can't a person have a little privacy in this family?"

"Sure," Mom answered. "But not when your idea of private is locking everyone else out of the bathroom in a one-bathroom apartment. Here - " A towel appeared through the shower curtain. "Dry yourself off."

I took the towel. "I'm not coming out," I insisted. "And I'm not going to school."

"Listen," Mom said. "When you're an adult and working hard and earning piles of money, then you can stay home and do whatever you want. Until then, you are a child and your job is to go to school. Now if something is bothering you about school, then we need to talk. But staying in the shower the rest of your life is not acceptable in this house. Get it?"

I sighed. "Got it."

"Good." Mom's voice softened. "Then dry off, get dressed and come out for breakfast. I'll make you some more hot muffins and we'll talk. Just you and me, okay?"

"Okay," I said. "The water was starting to get cold, anyway."

Mom moaned. "Oh, dear. Wait'll Juliet hears about that!"

I heard the door shut, but I didn't move. I just stood there, staring at my lizard-fingers and my prune-toes. Mom's a good listener. She was really understanding two years ago when I almost flunked math. But I wasn't sure she'd understand *this*.

I poked at the Ivory soap. It had kind of oozed over the edge of the soap dish like the insides of a hot, smushed Twinkie. My insides felt the same way. I didn't want to go to school. I'd rather eat that soap. I'd rather have shriveled skin that falls off. I'd rather listen to Juliet scream at me for three whole days. Anything would be better than going to school and standing in front of...The Eye.

CHAPTER TWO

"I don't like this," Mom said, as we sped along the road in our Toyota. "I don't like sending you to school when I know you're upset about something."

"So let me stay home," I answered.

"Uh-uh. Not till you tell me what's going on." Mom glanced at me. I was sitting next to her, holding a napkin wrapped around two English muffins with peanut butter. No time to eat breakfast at home. No time to walk to school with my friends. My World Record shower had made me very, very late.

"Jeffrey?"

"I don't want to talk about it," I said, and stared out the window. I could see the American flag flying above the school, just a few blocks away. My insides felt all smushed again. I clutched at the napkin. The English muffins had gotten cold and hard.

"Maybe you'll want to talk tonight?" Mom asked hopefully.

"Maybe."

"Don't you think you'll feel better once you do?"

"Maybe."

Mom sighed.

A few minutes later, we reached the school. Mom parked in front, letting the engine idle.

"Wait, Jeffrey," she said, rummaging through her purse. "You'll need a note." She found a pen and scribbled something on a scrap of paper. She folded it and handed it to me. "I hope your day goes all right, honey."

"Couldn't I go to work with you?" I asked. Mom's a checker at a grocery store. "I could rearrange the shelves. See, I've got this great system. We line up all the good stuff alphabetically. Peanut butter, Pizza, Popcorn, Pretzels..."

Mom smiled, but shook her head. "No, Jeffrey."

"This might be a good day for me to see the dentist," I said. "I think I can feel a cavity. I think I can feel two cavities." I opened my mouth and poked around at my teeth with my tongue. "I ink I an eel *eee* aieez."

Mom laughed. "What?"

"Three cavities," I replied.

"Nice try, Jeffrey. But you just saw Dr. Rathbone last month."

"I don't feel so good," I went on. I touched my forehead. "I think I have a fever. I'm very hot."

"Of course you're hot," Mom answered. "You just spent 38 minutes standing in a hot shower."

"No, Mom. I'm sick. Really. I'll bet I have a disease."

Mom leaned across me and opened the door. "Out!" she said.

"*Okay.*" I leaped out of the car and slammed the door.

"You forgot your books," Mom called.

I pulled open the door. Grabbed my books.

"And your muffins," Mom said.

"I'm much too sick to eat," I answered, trying to make my voice sound weak and quivery.

"Well, I hope you feel better soon. See you tonight, sweetheart." Mom waved, but I just slammed the door again and turned away. I didn't even say goodbye.

I walked toward my classroom real slow and cool, kicking a stone as I went, trying to act as if I didn't care about Mom as much as she didn't care about me. Huh. I knew she wouldn't understand. I'll bet she'd even written an embarrassing note. Something like, "Dear Miss Simmons: Jeffrey is late today because he locked himself in the bathroom and tried to take a World Record shower because he was afraid to come to school."

I ducked around a corner of the building and

opened Mom's note. It read:

"Dear Miss Simmons:
Please excuse Jeffrey for being late. We
had some plumbing problems at home this
morning.
Sincerely,
Mrs. McMillan."

Hmm. Maybe Mom wasn't so bad after all.

I reached the door to Room 5. That's my
classroom. That's where The Eye waited for me.

I touched the doorknob. It felt cool against my
hot hand. My heart started to pound. Then I knew
why my insides felt so smushed. There was a
rhinoceros doing jumping jacks in my stomach. I
could picture him in a pair of jogging shorts and
two pairs of tennis shoes. He was sweating, and
snorting, "Okay, only eight hundred more jumping
jacks to go!"

I wanted to run away. I wanted to hide. I looked

around for a good place, when suddenly the door opened.

"Jeffrey! You startled me!" Miss Simmons said. She smiled. "I was just about to take the attendance sheet to the office. I'd marked you absent. Well, I'm glad you're here. We would've missed you. It's a special day, remember?"

I nodded, looking down at my shoes.

Miss Simmons put her arm around me. "Come on in, Jeffrey. We're ready to get started."

The Eye. Miss Simmons was talking about The Eye.

I took a deep breath and let her steer me into the classroom.

CHAPTER THREE

Sliding into my seat, I glanced quickly around the classroom. My best friend, Teresa Mendoza, mouthed "hello" to me around her usual wad of bubble gum. No sign of The Eye. I wasn't fooled, though. It probably lurked in the closet, knowing today was the day - the day it would get me.

I put my books away and tried to listen to Miss Simmons talk about current events. Suddenly, something white sailed over my shoulder and landed on my desk. A note. Had to be from Craig Zeisloft. Craig is my other best friend. He sits behind me and writes me at least 85 notes a day.

I opened Craig's note. It said:

"Yo, Jeffrey!

Howzit? Why were you so late? Did you have a fight with Juliet? Did you have *two* fights with Juliet? Are you sick of all these questions? Are you freaked-out about today? Me, too. I don't want the whole world to see me like *this*.

Later,
Craig."

On the back of Craig's note I wrote:
"Hi.

In answer to your questions: Not great. Because. Yes. Yes. Yes. I don't blame you.

Jeffrey."

I turned to slip Craig the note and did a double-take. Even though he'd looked like that for five days, I still wasn't used to it. You see, Craig is *orange*.

This is what happened.

More than anything, Craig wants to be a hot surfer. He's never surfed before, but he reads all the surf mags, wears Aloha shirts (even when it's snowing), and owns every Beach Boys album ever recorded. Now there are only three things Craig needs to become a hot surfer:

1. A surfboard
2. A beach
3. A suntan

Craig has bright red hair (as red as a stop sign), and white skin. Craig *hates* his white skin, so last Sunday he smeared a whole bottle of that fake tanning stuff all over his body. Something went wrong. Very wrong. Craig isn't the least bit tan. Instead, he looks like a walking, orange popsicle.

Miss Simmons' voice interrupted my thoughts.

"All right, let's get started on our new project," she said.

The class gave some moans, groans and mumbles.

Craig, Teresa and I did all three.

"As I explained yesterday," Miss Simmons went on, "each one of you will give a short speech on how to do something. Your speech can be on anything at all. How to write a letter, how to bake brownies, how to care for a pet..."

"Miss Simmons, Miss Simmons!" Richard Jensen interrupted. He waved both arms in the air. "Miss Simmons, I have a great idea for a 'How-To' speech. Are you ready for this? It's called, 'How to Make Your Teacher Mad.' "

A few kids laughed. Richard sat back, his arms folded across his chest. He smiled the way Juliet did once, when she sneaked into our parents' closet and found a whole pile of Christmas presents with her name on them.

"I think that's a very interesting idea, Richard," Miss Simmons answered. "You know, I was thinking of giving a similar speech. It's called,

'How to Make Your Students Regret They Ever Made You Mad.' "

Craig and I snickered. Richard just hunched his shoulders and scowled at his desk.

"As I was saying," Miss Simmons went on, "there are two reasons why I think it's important for everyone to know how to give a speech. Number one, explaining how to do something will help you think in a more clear and organized way. And number two, all of you, at some point when you get older, will have to talk in front of a group of people. That can often make you feel a little nervous. So if you practice speaking to groups now, it will seem less scary later."

Maybe I won't have to do this, I thought desperately. Maybe the Governor will suddenly call to say I've won the lottery. Maybe a stampede of wild rhinoceros will come crashing through the classroom. Maybe...

"To help you to see how well you're doing," Miss Simmons said, gliding over to the closet, "I'll be using this."

I clutched the sides of my chair. Oh, no. This is it. She's pulling out The Eye.

Miss Simmons opened the closet door. Carefully, she took out a huge tripod. Perched on top of it was a video camera.

The Eye.

I shuddered and looked away.

"This week," Miss Simmons continued, "I'll be filming each of you as you practice reading aloud to the class. The video will show if you're standing nice and tall, and if you have good eye contact with your audience. Now let's see, who will go first?"

A note sailed over my shoulder. I opened it with shaky fingers. It read:

"Don't panic, Jeffrey! Miss Simmons
always starts at the beginning or
the end of the alphabet. You
probably won't get called on until
tomorrow."

I gave a huge sigh of relief.

"I think," Miss Simmons said, "that I'll choose someone from the middle of the alphabet today. Jeffrey McMillan, we'll start with you."

CHAPTER FOUR

I felt numb all over. Except where Richard Jensen was jabbing me in the arm with his sharp pencil.

"Hey, Snail Slime," he said. Jab. "You deaf or something?" Jab, jab. "Miss Simmons just called on you."

I looked over at Richard. I'd never liked him. In third grade, he had sneaky eyes. Always peeking at my math tests to see if I'd flunked another one. In fourth grade, he added a sneaky mouth. Started making up names, like Broccoli Breath and Diaper Brain, for kids he hated. And now he had that sneaky pencil.

Jab, jab, jab.

"Quit it," I whispered through clenched teeth.

"Make me!"

"Jeffrey," Miss Simmons said, "we're waiting. Stand at the front of the class, please, and read a few paragraphs from your library book. I'll tell you when to stop."

I took a book about rhinoceroses from my desk and moved slowly to the front of the room. My legs felt like cooked spaghetti. My heart beat in funny jerks.

"Stand right there," Miss Simmons said. "No, face *us*, Jeffrey. That's fine. Now remember, lots of eye contact."

I lifted my head and stared at The Eye. It stared back. It never blinked. It looked black and cold and mean.

My heart jerked faster. My tongue felt dry and wooden, like an old popsicle stick. Hot prickles ran up my neck.

The Eye kept staring. It seemed to grow wider,

blacker. It was going to get me, suck me in...

"Anytime you're ready, Jeffrey," Miss Simmons said.

"Lights, camera, action!" shouted Richard Jensen. It almost sounded like he'd said, "Ready, aim, fire."

My hands shook. My knees wobbled. Would I be able to talk? Or would I freeze the way I did last year when...

Don't think about that. Don't.

I pulled my gaze away from The Eye and stared down at my book. The first word on the page was "rhinoceros." It's a nice word, I thought. I like it. I've said it a thousand, maybe a million times. I can say it again. It's easy.

I opened my mouth and said, "Gleek."

Richard Jensen snickered.

I swallowed at the dryness in my throat and tried again. "Gurple," I said.

More kids laughed.

"Gleek, gurple, griff," I said.

My face got hot. The Eye kept staring.

"Are you all right, Jeffrey?" Miss Simmons asked.

"Garf," I answered.

Richard Jensen laughed so hard he fell off his chair.

"Richard, what are you doing on the floor?" Miss Simmons demanded.

"Sorry," Richard said, holding his stomach. "I've had a serious chair malfunction."

I'd like to malfunction your head, I thought.

"Richard, please take your seat," Miss Simmons instructed. "And Jeffrey, perhaps you'd like to get a drink of water?"

I nodded. Couldn't trust my voice. My throat and face felt on fire.

"Teresa Mendoza, you're next," Miss Simmons said. "But first, you need to throw away that impressive wad of gum."

Head bent, rhinoceros book clutched to my chest, I hurried down the aisle. Were the kids still

26

laughing at me? Staring at me?

"Way to go, Cow Cud," Richard Jensen said with a smirk, when I passed his desk.

I glared at him and sped out the door.

In the hall, I took thirteen big gulps of water from the drinking fountain. My stomach swelled out and kind of sloshed around, but at least my tongue didn't feel like a popsicle stick any more. My heart slowed down, too.

Miss Simmons stuck her head out the door. "Feeling better?" she asked.

"Sorta," I answered.

Miss Simmons came outside, shutting the door softly behind her. "We're taking a short break," she said. "Teresa blew quite a bubble before throwing out her gum. Unfortunately, it exploded in her hair, her eyelashes, her library book..." Miss Simmons sighed. "Anyway, I wanted to loan you this."

She handed me a book. The title was *How to Give a Speech: A Guide for Kids.*

"I'd like you to read chapter ten," Miss Simmons continued. "It's about dealing with stage fright."

"I don't have stage fright," I said quickly. "In there I had, you know, just something stuck in my throat. It's gone. I'm okay now." I coughed once to prove it.

Miss Simmons' left eye winked funny. I remembered that wink from when she taught my class in third grade. Miss Simmons' left eye always does that when she thinks we've told a lie. I wasn't really lying. There are lots of things stuck in my throat. My tongue, my tonsils...

"Hmmm," Miss Simmons said. "Well, I'd like you to read that chapter anyway, Jeffrey. Just in case you experience stage fright in the future." She squeezed my shoulder. "Join us again when you're ready. I'd better make sure Teresa's been de-gummed. " She hurried back inside.

I stood alone in the hall, staring at the book. I turned to chapter ten. The first line began,

"Unfortunately, there is no shot or pill that will prevent stage fright. However..."

I slammed the book shut. How could it help me? I was doomed. Doomed to be scared of The Eye. Doomed to hear the kids laugh at me. Doomed to act dumb and stupid, the way I had last year...the way I had today.

Doomed, doomed, doomed.

CHAPTER FIVE

The recess bell rang a minute later.

The door flew open. Teresa charged over to me, linked her arm through mine and dragged me down the hall. "Come on," she said, snapping her gum.

Craig followed us to the playground to our favorite Tuesday hang-out. They bake peanut butter cookies on Tuesday, so we sit directly beneath the cafeteria window. A hot peanutty smell floats out slow and thick and rich, and makes our noses glad to be alive.

"What happened to you in class?" Teresa demanded. "I've never seen you act so *weird*."

"I have," Craig said.

"Thanks," I mumbled.

"Well, it's true," Craig insisted. He jerked his orange head toward Teresa. "You never told her?"

"Told me what?" Teresa asked, hands on her hips.

I shrugged. "She was on vacation."

"Told me *what*?" Teresa repeated.

"Besides, I just wanted to forget about it," I continued. "I didn't think it would happen again."

"What! What!" Teresa shouted. Her jaws were chomping in warp drive. Teresa is the best bubble gum chewer in the whole world. Probably because she's had so much practice. There are only three times a day when Teresa doesn't chew bubble gum. They are:

1. When she's eating breakfast.
2. When she's eating lunch.
3. When she's eating dinner.

Teresa says she even chews gum when she's sleeping, but I don't believe her. She probably just tucks it in her cheek.

"*Jeffrey*," Teresa said. "Tell me!"

"It's a long story."

"I don't mind."

"It happened a long, long time ago. Last summer."

Teresa glared at me.

"Okay, okay." I took a deep breath. "Here goes..."

* * * * *

I will never forget that night. It was the first time I ever saw The Eye.

I was home watching a Twilight Zone show on TV. Mom and Dad had gone to a movie. They said I could stay alone since Juliet was babysitting across the hall for some people named the Halstons.

The Halstons were kinda quiet and mysterious. They always wore safari clothes. You know, camouflage pants with canteens hooked to their belts. And they never talked to anyone. Or smiled. They weren't mean or anything, just different. They liked to hike up the stairs of our apartment building instead of taking the elevator, and we live on the 18th floor! And sometimes, late at night, we'd hear strange noises coming from their apartment. Mrs. Halston explained that they had a new baby, but I'd never heard a baby sound like *that*.

Anyway, the Halstons had called Juliet and said they wanted to go out for an hour. They offered to pay her ten dollars if she'd sit for their new baby, Edgar. Strange thing was, they didn't want Juliet to play with him or anything. "Under *n o circumstances* are you to go in Edgar's room," they told her. "What if he cries or needs changing or something?" Juliet asked. "That won't happen," the Halstons promised. "We just fed and changed him. He needs his sleep, so don't you dare disturb him."

Juliet agreed. For ten dollars, she would've agreed to stop yelling at me for a whole hour.

So anyway, there I sat, watching my favorite Twilight Zone episode. Juliet had only been gone a few minutes, when the phone rang.

I snatched up the receiver. "Hello," I said.

"Daaa-aaad!" Juliet whispered roughly.

"Dad's not here, Juliet."

"Get Mom, then - quick!"

"Mom's not here either. They went to the movies. Why are you whispering?"

"Jeffrey, you've got to come over here!"

"I can't. I'm watching Twilight Zone."

"Jeffrey," Juliet hissed, "something weird is going on in this place and I'm *scared*. If you don't come over by the time I count to ten, you'll be in big trouble. Do you know what that means? It means you're history! Are you listening, Jeffrey?"

The phone went dead.

The Twilight Zone music went *Dee dee dee dee, dee dee dee dee*. My neck got all prickly. I threw down the phone and made it to the Halston's apartment, by the count of three.

"Are you all right?" I asked Juliet. "We got cut off!"

"I hung up," she said. "Come here, look at this." She pulled me into the kitchen and opened the refrigerator. Inside was a baby bottle. It stood about two feet tall and one foot wide.

I whistled. "Wow, Edgar must be one big baby."

"And that's not all," Juliet said. "Listen to this."

We stood outside of Edgar's room. We heard funny breathing and snuffling. And loud, heavy footsteps. And then a muffled crunching.

"Sounds like Edgar's eating the curtains," I murmured.

"That's no baby," Juliet whispered. "I'll bet they've got a...a monster in there!"

My neck prickled again. I didn't want Juliet to know I was scared, so I said, "Maybe we should peek inside."

Juliet clutched my arm. "We can't! I won't get my ten dollars if we do."

"The Halstons will never know," I replied. "Besides, Edgar sounds like he has a cold. Maybe he needs his nose blown. You might get in trouble for neglecting a sick baby. I'm gonna check." Slowly, I opened the door.

Something big and grey stood there. It was about the size of a VW Beetle. We stared at each other for a few seconds. When it blinked at me, I slammed the door.

"Whatisit, whatisit?" Juliet asked.

I swallowed hard. "Juliet, I regret to inform you," I began slowly, "that you're babysitting for a...a rhinoceros."

Juliet fainted.

At first, I wasn't sure what to do. I knew our apartment building didn't allow pets, so finally I called the police to report a rhinoceros-in-a-bedroom. Then I poured a glass of water on Juliet's face, to wake her up. While she was still sputtering and coughing, the police arrived. And the newspaper reporters. And the film crews.

They discovered that Edgar wasn't a rhinoceros after all. He was a baby elephant. The Halstons had *stolen* him from the city zoo.

"You're quite the hero, son," one policeman told me.

I puffed up, feeling proud.

"It was *my* babysitting job," Juliet grumbled.

"We'll have the Halstons arrested," the policeman continued.

"And I'll never get my ten dollars," Juliet grumbled.

"We'd like to interview you for the eleven o'clock news, Jeffrey," said a man with a video camera. He turned on some bright lights.

"You mean I'll be on television?" I asked.

"Uh-huh."

"In front of thousands of people?"

"Millions," the man answered.

"Don't mess up," Juliet said with a sneer.

The man fiddled with the camera. I started to feel nervous. What if I said something stupid in front of millions of people? Would my friends laugh at me?

The man turned on the camera. A reporter shoved a microphone under my nose. "I'm standing here with Jeffrey McMillan," he announced, "who tonight discovered the whereabouts of Edgar the Elephant. Tell the audience, Jeffrey, exactly how this came about."

I lifted my head and stared at the video camera. It stared back at me like a big, black eye. It never blinked. It just stared and stared...

My heart beat in funny jerks. My tongue felt dry and wooden.

The Eye kept staring.

"Jeffrey?" the reporter said.

I opened my mouth and...froze. I couldn't say a word. Millons of people were watching me stand there with my mouth open, and I couldn't say a word!

Juliet snickered.

"Well," the reporter said, "it seems even our

hero has been left speechless at finding an elephant in the bedroom."

The video man laughed. I heard a policeman chuckle. They were laughing at me. I was a failure.

With my face burning, I ran past The Eye, out of the apartment, across the hall, into our apartment, into my bedroom and slammed the door.

CHAPTER SIX

"Wow," Teresa said. "That's an awful story, Jeffrey. You musta felt *terrible*."

"Oh, he did," Craig agreed. "Especially when he saw himself on the morning and evening news."

"Richard Jensen called me the Moronic Marvel for a week," I mumbled.

"I think it's time we explored Jeffrey's options," Teresa announced.

"What?" Craig and I asked, confused.

Teresa sighed. "We have to figure a way to get Jeffrey out of giving a speech." She took another stick of gum from her pocket and added it to the wad in her mouth. She chewed juicily for a few seconds. "Okay, Jeffrey. First, you could run away from home."

"Uh-uh. No way." I shook my head, remembering. Two years ago, Craig, Teresa and I had tried to run away to Africa after I flunked a math test. Problem was, we discovered that Africa is across the Atlantic Ocean, about three thousand miles away, and we would've had to *swim*.

"Okay, second," Teresa went on, "just tell Miss Simmons that you're not giving a speech. Instead, offer to write a 30-page report on the extreme importance of neat homework."

Craig grabbed his throat and made fake choking sounds.

"Teresa," I began, "Miss Simmons said *everyone* has to give a speech. So if I don't, I'll get an F. And my parents will get so mad they won't let me watch TV for a month."

"True," Teresa said. "All right, how 'bout if you tell Miss Simmons you're allergic to speeches? You could sneeze a lot and get a note from your doctor and..."

43

Just then, Richard Jensen cruised by with two of his friends.

"Well, if it isn't the Moronic Marvel," Richard said with a sneaky grin. "Slower than a molting caterpillar! Weaker than a baby's toenail! Able to trip over his own tongue with a single bound!" Richard and his friends laughed, and started to saunter away.

My face got hot. I stared at the ground, my hands balled into tight fists.

"No brains, no headaches," Teresa shouted after them.

"Yeah, you should know, Spinach Face," Richard shot over his shoulder.

Teresa shrugged. "Just ignore them, Jeffrey. Now, getting back to your options..."

"Thanks for your help, Teresa, but - " I took a deep breath. "But I have to give this speech."

"You're not going to do it just because of what Richard said, are you?" Craig asked.

"No. Yes. No, it's because I have to stand up to

the Eye. Face to face. Eye to eye. That's the only way to beat it."

"But how, Jeffrey?" Teresa demanded.

I held up the book Miss Simmons had given me. "I've got a little help. The rest I'll have to figure out myself."

* * * * *

After school, I hurried straight home. The door of Dad's den was closed, and I could hear the click-clicka-click of his typewriter. Dad is almost finished writing his latest book. It breaks his concentration if he's disturbed in the middle of a thought, so we have a system. I'm supposed to knock on his door three times, just to let him know I'm home. Then when Dad's ready for a break, he comes out to say hi.

I knocked on his door, then went to the kitchen to make my favorite afternoon snack: two peanut butter sandwiches. I took them and Miss Simmons' book to my room. There's nothing better than rolling a thick, gooey, peanutty bite of sandwich around in your mouth to help you to think.

I spent the whole afternoon chewing, and reading the chapter on stage fright. The chapter said some pretty good things. I made a list of the most important. This is what they were:

1. Choose a topic that's important to you; something you do very well. If you enjoy playing soccer, you'll enjoy talking about it, too.
2. Practice, practice, practice! If you know what you're going to say, you'll feel more confident about your presentation.
3. Concentrate on your speech, not on yourself. You have a choice: to spend time and energy thinking about being scared, or giving a lively speech.
4. Before your speech, try a few stretching exercises to relieve tension.

5. If you make a mistake, don't let the audience know. Try to make it part of the show.

"Jeffrey!" I heard my mother call. She must've gotten home from work. "Jeffrey, will you help me make a salad for dinner?"

"Sure," I called back, and shut my book.

In the kitchen, I found Juliet doing homework at the kitchen table. Mom handed me a bowl and some vegetables from the refrigerator.

I washed my hands and started tearing lettuce. Mom chopped tomatoes. She also kept looking at me out of the corner of her eye, like she was waiting for me to say something.

"So," she said at last.

"So," I echoed.

Silence.

"Well," she said brightly.

"Well," I repeated.

"So," Mom began again. "Have you decided if you'd like to discuss what's bothering you about school?"

I glanced at Juliet.

She was staring at me. Instantly, she buried her nose in her homework. "I'm not listening," she said. "Just pretend I'm not here."

"Jeffrey?" prompted Mom.

I sighed. "I have to give a speech, Mom. In front of a video camera."

"Ah, ha!" Juliet said. "No wonder you didn't want to get out of the shower this morning."

"You said you weren't listening!" I shot angrily.

"Well, I couldn't help overhearing..."

"Juliet," Mom said, "if you can't sit quietly, you'll have to leave the room."

"My lips," Juliet replied with a zipping motion, "are sealed. But tell Jeffrey to stop mutilating the lettuce. It's so shredded, we'll have to drink it with a straw."

I tried to tear the lettuce in larger pieces.

"Go on, Jeffrey," Mom said. "Tell me more about your speech."

I told Mom about Miss Simmons' book, and the list of important ways to keep from getting nervous.

"So first," I said, "I have to come up with something I do really well. I've been thinking and thinking. But I'm not good at anything."

"Sure you are," Juliet said. "You could give a great speech on how to get As in math."

I glared at her. I don't get Fs on my math tests anymore, but I certainly don't get As. "Very funny, Juliet," I said. "I think I'll give a speech on the care and feeding of a rhinoceros-for-a-sister."

"Moooo-ooom," Juliet screeched. "Did you hear what Jeffrey called me? He called me a - "

"Goodbye, Juliet," Mom said.

"But, Mom - "

"I said, *goodbye*, Juliet."

"Oh, all right." Juliet sighed, scooped up her homework and flounced from the room.

"That's better," Mom said. "Now, Jeffrey, tell me what Craig's speech is about."

"How to Surf."

"Uh-huh. And Teresa's?"

"How to Blow Bubbles."

"Of course." Mom smiled. "Hmmm. Well, Jeffrey, you're an excellent speller. A real pro at video games. You bake a mean peanut butter cookie. And grandma says you write the nicest thank-you notes."

Bor-ring. I'd put everyone to sleep with a speech about *that*. Then Miss Simmons would be sure to give me an F.

"Those are all good ideas," I said politely. "I'll think about them and let you know."

"Good. Glad I could help," Mom said. "And remember, when you're ready, Dad and I would love to be your practice audience."

Audience. I suddenly thought of the kids watching me. And The Eye. "Okay. Thanks," I said, hoping Mom couldn't hear the nervousness in my voice. Or the nervous gurglings in my stomach. I finished making the salad, then headed straight for the bathroom.

Just as I reached the door, Juliet scooted in front of me.

"Oh, no you don't," she said. "Me first."

"Juliet, I really have to go," I said. "I'll be out in two seconds."

"No way. The last time you were in there, you didn't come out for almost a week."

"But I was here first!"

"Tough. I'm not taking any chances."

"Juliet!" I starting hopping up and down on one foot.

"Okay," Juliet said. "I'll make you a deal. You let me use the bathroom first, and I'll tell you the perfect way to give a speech without getting nervous."

I stopped hopping. "Really? How?"

Juliet stared right into my eyes and whispered: "Use visual aids." Then she scooted into the bathroom.

"Wait a minute," I cried, grabbing her arm.

"What do you mean 'visual aids'?"

Juliet sighed noisily. "You know, *visual aids*. Like, if Craig is doing a speech about surfing, he'll bring stuff like a surfboard, surf wax, a shock cord, bucket of salt water, things like that. Visual aids distract the audience from looking at you. They also help you to remember what you're going to say next in your speech. Then you don't have to worry about freezing up, forgetting what you're supposed to say. Now excuse me, I have to wash my hair."

The door slammed in my face. I dragged back to my room. To forget about needing to use the bathroom, I stuffed the last bite of peanut butter sandwich into my mouth.

Choose a topic that's important to you...something you do very well.

The words swirled around in my head as I swirled the peanut butter around in my mouth. What was important to me? What did I do really well?

I swallowed. The peanut butter tasted creamy and delicious.

Then I knew.

I felt a smile spreading across my face. My idea was perfect. Easy. Something I did every day. Something I loved doing every day. And I could use visual aids, too. This might even be *fun*.

I leaped into my desk chair, grabbed a pencil, and began writing my speech.

CHAPTER SEVEN

A week later, I was ready to face The Eye.

"What's all this stuff?" Craig asked as he, Teresa and I walked to school.

"Yeah," Teresa said, poking at my overstuffed book pack. "What's *in* there?"

"My lunch, a thermos of milk, and - "I paused mysteriously " - visual aids. For my speech, you know."

"Cool," Craig said knowingly, but he looked confused.

"Jeffrey, won't you *please* tell us what your speech is about?" Teresa begged. "You know what we're doing."

I shook my head. "I want it to be a surprise."

"Did you figure out a way to beat The Eye?" Craig asked.

"Sure," I answered. We stopped at the school crosswalk, waiting for the light to change. "First, I picked a 'How-To' topic I'm good at, which you'll find out about after morning recess. I'm giving my speech first."

"First?!" Craig and Teresa shouted together.

"Uh-huh," I said with a grin. "That way, I'll get it over with quick. I didn't want to sit in class all morning, worrying about when my turn would come."

"Smart," Teresa said.

"I also practiced my speech about a zillion times this week," I said. "Mom, Dad and Juliet were my audience."

"Juliet?" Craig whistled. "Jeffrey, you're either very brave or very dumb."

"Brave," I said. The light changed. We crossed the street. "I figured Juliet made a good Richard Jensen. I knew if I didn't freeze up around her, I wouldn't around Richard. Or The Eye."

"What did Juliet think of your speech?" Teresa asked.

"She said, 'Not bad, for a little nerd.' That means she loved it."

The school bell rang. We raced into the building.

Attendance, current events, math. For that first hour of school, I felt pretty calm. But as recess time got closer, my stomach started to twitch. My brain was twitching, too.

In just a few minutes, you'll be standing in front of The Eye. It'll suck you in and spit you out! You can't do this, you can't!

Yes, I can , I argued back, and leaped up as soon as the recess bell rang. I remembered something else from Miss Simmons' book. "Before your speech, try a few exercises to relieve tension."

I ran around the backstop six times.

Then I did eighty-four jumping jacks.

Next I did fifty sit-ups, twenty chin-ups and two

handstands. My body felt like two rhinoceroses had square danced on it. But at least I wasn't tense.

"Jeffrey," Miss Simmons said when recess ended, "we're ready when you are." She switched on The Eye.

I wiped a trickle of sweat from my face, grabbed my book pack and headed for the front of the room.

"Show us your stuff, Slobber Nose," Richard Jensen said.

I ignored him. Carefully, I unpacked and arranged all the visual aids on a small table. Then I faced The Eye.

It stared back at me. Black. Unblinking. Mean.

My stomach quivered. My knees trembled. My hands shook. And those awful prickles spidered up my back. Oh, no. Not again. I was going to freeze. I was going to make a fool of myself. I was ...

Words from the speech book suddenly flashed across my mind. "You have a choice: to spend time thinking about being scared, or giving a lively speech."

I pulled my gaze away from The Eye. I faced the class, took a deep breath and started talking.

"Peanut butter is my favorite food. In fact, there's nothing I like better for lunch than a smooth, creamy, peanutty, peanut butter sandwich. All my friends used to love peanut butter sandwiches, too. But lately, I've seen some of them trading sandwiches for chicken legs or bologna. I've even spotted a few kids throwing their sandwiches away! This is sad. I think the problem is that some kids just don't know how to make a perfect peanut butter sandwich. So today I'm going to show you."

Richard Jensen snickered. Everyone else sat quietly. They weren't snoring or fidgeting or whispering. They were listening!

"First," I went on, "you need to start with the proper ingredients. A loaf of whole wheat bread, because it's healthy. One stick of butter - not margarine - that's softened, for better spreading. One flat knife. One plate. One jar of old-fashioned peanut butter, creamy style or super-chunk. A napkin. And one tape recorder."

A few kids exchanged glances. Craig's eyebrows went up, almost touching his red hair. I heard someone whisper, "A tape recorder?"

"Now," I continued, "take two slices of bread from the loaf, and arrange them neatly on your plate. Then, using your knife, smooth some butter on both slices, making sure to cover all the corners." I demonstrated, then opened the jar of peanut butter. "Next, stir the peanut butter to blend all the oils. Now this next part is very important. You need to set the proper mood before you can spread the peanut butter correctly. So select a cassette tape from your collection...insert it into the recorder...press the start button, and..."

The steady beat and finger-snapping music of Michael Jackson's latest song filled the classroom.

Tapping my foot, rocking my hips, I began to smooth peanut butter onto the bread. My arm swooped and swirled. The knife flashed under the fluorescent lights as I dipped it again and again into the peanut butter jar.

Kids laughed. Rocked their heads. Clapped to the music.

Dip, swirl. Dip, swirl. Whiffs of peanut butter rose up and tickled my nose. I whirled. I twirled. I grinned. I swirled. Then, humming to the music, I placed the bread together. With a final swoop of the knife, I cut the sandwich in two. The music ended. The sandwich was made.

"Whooo!" someone shouted.

Kids were giggling, humming. Miss Simmons beamed.

"And now - " I paused, breathless, waiting for the noise to die down. "And now, the last thing you need to do is *taste* your peanut butter sandwich."

I raised the sandwich to my lips, closed my eyes, and took the biggest, most humungous bite I'd ever taken in my life.

My mouth seemed to scream with happiness. The sandwich tasted perfect, all rich and thick and peanutty-sweet. I chewed blissfully for a few seconds, then opened my eyes. Time to finish my speech.

I tried to swallow. I tried again. Nothing happened! My throat was welded shut with that humungous wad of peanut butter. I couldn't swallow. I couldn't talk. I couldn't do anything!

I turned and looked at The Eye. It stared back, wide and black, like a big laughing mouth. It had won. The Eye had won again. I was standing in front of it, frozen, just like before. Nothing would ever change.

The seconds ticked by. The peanut butter in my mouth wouldn't budge. Soon the kids would realize something was wrong, and start to laugh. Richard Jensen would call me Cement Mouth for the rest of my life. Miss Simmons would give me an F. I was doomed, and all because of one little mistake!

Mistake.

"If you make a mistake, don't let the audience know", Miss Simmons' book had said. "Make the mistake part of the show!"

Then I knew what to do.

I held up a finger. The kids waited quietly. I dug into my bookpack, and pulled out the thermos of milk. Quickly, I unscrewed the top and took a long, cold gulp. Then I chewed a bit more and took another long gulp. The peanut butter started to loosen. I chewed again and took one last swallow. The peanut butter slid down my throat.

"Ahhhhh!" I said, and wiped my mouth with the napkin. "And remember, even the most perfect peanut butter sandwich isn't really perfect unless you have an ice cold glass of milk to help wash it down. Thank you."

I bowed. The class broke into wild applause. Craig gave me the thumbs-up signal. Teresa blew a tremendous bubble. Miss Simmons just smiled and smiled.

I bowed again and turned toward The Eye. We stared at each other for a long minute, face to face, eye to eye. And then, I winked.

The End